Olivia

Jack

Lily

Evie

Kitchen towels

Cereals

Water

Bread

Muffins

Bread rolls

Eggs

We're at the supermarket. The little bears have moved some things around. Can you spot which things are in the wrong places? Where do they belong?

Dog

Hat

Well done! Everyone looks happy now. But can you find Olivia Bear and her pink sandal?

Sheep

Goose

Chicken

I asked the little bears to go quietly through the farm but they simply ran wild. Can you please put these animals and objects back where they belong?

Cow

Hay

Wheel

Mask

Ball

Goodness me! There's a funfair on
the playing field. The little bears
went crashing through and have
knocked things all over the place.
Do please help me to tidy up.

Cup

Balloon

Saddle

Steering
wheel

Paper plate

Deckchair

Banana

Now we're at the lake. The little bears began to set out the picnic but then ran away to play, leaving a mess.

Towel

Crisps

Can you help me tidy
up, please?

Hurrah! We're eating our picnic at last. But can you find Jack Bear and the blue sunglasses he was wearing?

It's time to walk home now. But I can't carry all these towels. Can you please give each little bear the correct towel. And hand them each their own backpack, too.

What a very exciting time we've had! Now
everything has been put away and at last I can sit
down and read. Do please come and visit us again.